MIRROR IMAGES

by
Susan Satterfield

Mirror Images
Susan Satterfield
First Edition Copyright © Susan Satterfield, 2002
Second Edition Copyright © Susan Satterfield, 2016

Published by Yard Dog Press at Create Space

ISBN 978-1-937105-89-1

Mirror Images
Second Edition Copyright © Susan Satterfield, 2016

Yard Dog Press
710 W. Redbud Lane
Alma, AR   72921-7247

http://www.yarddogpress.com

Edited by Selina Rosen
Copy Editor & Technical Editor Lynn Rosen
Cover art by Rick Tinney

Printed in the United States of America
0 9 8 7 6 5 4 3 2 1

To all my family and friends
who helped me make it this far.

CHAPTER ONE
REFLECTIONS ON TIME AND SPACE

"It's-s-s time."

Tarel jumped even though he had heard the sibilant sounds of the voice hundreds of times since he became the Shopkeeper. It always affected him the same way. No matter how hard he tried, Tarel couldn't figure out how the *Klebba* contacted him. At this point, he didn't want to know. Not knowing made it feel magical, and Tarel enjoyed that feeling. Like always, the voice issued from the silvery surface of the wooden framed mirror that played such a large part in all of his adventures. He laughed to himself, remembering how frightened he had been the first time the *Klebba* had called him. Tarel had been on the verge of eradicating an entire planet of peaceful, caring creatures when the *Klebba* transferred his essence into the body he now wore. He remembered his anger at not being in control. He remembered his fear, a new feeling for him, when he realized that his fate rested in the slender hands of an enigmatic alien race. He remembered listening with disbelief, at first, and then with growing wonder as the *Klebba* explained to him *why* they had kidnapped him.

He remembered all of his adventures, and the different bodies he inhabited as he walked world after world helping to keep the fragile galaxy together and, in the process, finding a new purpose for himself. It had taken him longer to get used to this newly developed conscience than to the gnarly, ancient body he faced in the same mirror that was calling to him.

"I am here." The image in the mirror of the twisted body he now wore shivered and slowly faded into a mass of swirling colors. The colors finally merged into a vaguely humanoid shape that stepped through the silvery surface of the mirror. The being was surrounded by a field that pulsated with the same type of energy that lived within the mirror.

"You have come a long way s-s-since we firs-s-st met." The gentle hissing voice of the Klebba sounded almost musical to Tarel. The only clear characteristic he had ever been able to attribute to the creatures was their voices. Tarel couldn't quite see any specific features. He never did. The Klebba always appeared to him behind the safety of their energy screens since they could not survive in the same atmosphere as Tarel. He would never know what they truly looked like. Tarel wasn't even sure if he met different members of the Klebba each time, or if it was the same creature appearing to him over and over.

"With your help," Tarel responded, "I've learned much." Tarel tried to avoid looking directly at the creature. The field crawled with an energy that gave Tarel a headache if he looked at it too long, so he usually just tried to avoid looking at them. He looked around the main room of the store/vehicle. Storage compartments made of the same material as the mirror he now stood in front of were everywhere. Tarel saw his own image as well as the slowly shifting colors of the energy field surrounding the creature reflected hundreds of times around the deceptively large room. The walls of the structure they traveled in were curved slightly as the force field gently pushed at the outer surface, protecting the vehicle as it traveled through the wormhole created by the Klebba's machines. Even though the Klebba had attempted to explain the technology to Tarel, it was so sophisticated that it was impossible for him to grasp even the rudimentary elements. He knew it had something to do with black holes and the warping of space and time, but Tarel wasn't even sure he knew what *that* meant. Their technology even altered the shape of the shiny containers into any material goods he needed to accomplish his mission. Tarel could feel the nervous quivering begin in his stomach. It happened before every new mission. "What's the objective this time?" Tarel tried hard to keep his nervousness from affecting his speech.

Even though Tarel couldn't see it, he could feel the being's warm smile embrace him. "After all this-s-s time, you s-s-still feel apprehens-s-sive before a new as-s-signment. Tarel, we've offered this-s-s many times-s-s, but, once again, you know you can go home any time you like. Tarel, you have been rehabilitated for a long time. As-s-s always-s-s, the choice is yours-s-s."

Tarel shook his head. "No. There is nothing for me back home. You showed me what it truly means to be alive. I would rather stay where I can be of use."

The image nodded. "We could change your body to one that is-s-s more comfortable..."

"Once again, no." Tarel raised one misshapen arm and stretched his twisted fingers before him. "It reminds me of the terrible things I'm capable of doing, and what I don't ever want to become again. I'll wear it until you need me to be someone else. Until then, I'll keep it."

"As-s-s you wis-s-sh. You will not be wearing it for much longer anyway. We are nearing your next as-s-s-signment. Are you ready?"

Tarel nodded and braced himself. Even though he knew logically that it wouldn't hurt, imprinting always made him nervous. His body tingled as the bright, warm light now pulsating from the mirror washed over him. Pictures, words, emotions, all crowded into his brain as he relived someone else's life. Someone who was like he once was. Someone who carried in him the ability to save or destroy a world. Someone who must learn, like he finally did, that there is a price one must pay for the gift of life.

CHAPTER TWO
OLDE TOWNE

The storefront seemed quite ordinary. It fit in perfectly among all the other red brick buildings that had been the center of activity for the once nice neighborhood. While the area had obviously fallen on hard times, there were signs of life. There had obviously been an attempt to transform the dying neighborhood into a thriving bohemian area. It was an attempt that seemed on the verge of failure. All those who owned and worked at those establishments thought of themselves as being out of the ordinary, but in their struggle to recapture the free spirit born of the 60's, they only succeeded in copying what had been done in a number of locations throughout Middle America. It was the last bastion of hippies, New Agers, and those young suburbanites who wanted to somehow be "different" or, as was usually the case with many of the much younger patrons, those who wanted to shake up their parents. The problem was that the once flourishing quest for a nostalgic return to a free spirited age seemed to be fading as much of society appeared bent on acquiring the latest technological marvel to hit the marketplace.

There were a number of stores mixed in among the obviously empty buildings boasting "for lease or sale" signs. A head shop, appropriately called *Freaker's Palace*, which sold tie-dye shirts, used records, and an assortment of rock 'n roll memorabilia besides the usual pipes and "tobacco" products, inhabited the pharmacy that had at one time been the social center for the area. Sitting across the street from the newly arrived addition to the local business community, the *Freaker's Palace* had a jukebox that still played 45's sitting in one corner. The old soda fountain that had once been the social center for the community, now held boxes of slightly yellowed 8 X 10 photographs of Jim Morrison, Janis Joplin, and a multitude of other rock stars of the past. Black light posters, lava lamps, plasma lights, and strange glowing orbs were scattered around the store, giving an otherworldly glow to the dimly lit establishment.

Next door to *Freaker's Palace*, in what had once been the only grocery store around for miles, was *Altered States*, a tattoo parlor that also specialized in piercings. Its clientele ranged from the hard core bikers to the adventurous suburbanite. A sign in the front of the window declared *Altered States* was a clean, sterile tattoo studio specializing in custom work and cover-ups.

A bookstore, *The Mystic Market*, specializing in New Age materials, had taken up residence in the old dime store. Standing next door to the new business, it advertised an in-house psychic who read tarot cards or tea leaves to tell what the future held. In here, one could find out how to treat illness with common herbs and weeds, how to read someone's aura or how to locate those places of power, which could supposedly increase one's own psychic power. Its windows were filled with crystals on long leather strings. The window glass held bright paintings of eyes, weird geometric shapes, tarot cards, rainbows, and other mystic symbols.

The *Mystic Market* seemed bright and bizarre sitting next to the new shop. The new store appeared different because it seemed so ordinary. The front of the store was mostly clean red brick punctuated by freshly washed windows. Pieces of highly polished furnished and assorted bric-a-brac were prominently displayed in each of the four windows paired on either side of the frosted glass door. In many ways, the store looked like all the other antique/junk business found in virtually any town or city anywhere in the world. Even though it didn't boast the bright colors, rhythmic music, and forced persona emanating from the other establishments, it fit like it had always belonged among the other businesses. A simple wooden sign tastefully depicted the name of the store—*Tarel's Treasures and Antiques.* The name plaque hung from the rafters of a small porch that framed the doorway. A smaller sign hung just below: "Granters of wishes, fulfillers of dreams, not everything here may be what it seems." The business was easy to overlook because it did look so ordinary. When someone did spot the store, they had a hard time thinking about it. Its ordinariness made it hard to hold onto mentally. People knew it was there on some level, but somehow it seemed to vanish from their memories like rain puddles on a hot summer day.

This feeling was present in all the other shop owners who couldn't seem to remember exactly when the new store opened. As a matter of fact, they couldn't really remember the building being there at all. Some of them had vague memories of that location having been home to an empty lot, but every time anyone would make an attempt to discuss the store, the subject would somehow get changed and only later would they realize that the topic had slipped away from them. After awhile, everyone just accepted that the store was there. Some even claimed that it had always been there.

They all agreed that the owner of the store was a strange looking old man who nobody wanted to approach, let alone talk to.

Tarel, the "strange looking old man" that made everyone in Old Towne nervous, was getting everything ready so he could open in time for his first customer. He double-checked his supply of receipts and delivery forms. Then shoving a strand of long gray hair back toward his lanky ponytail, he hurried with a weird listing gait to the front door, unlocking it. After flipping over the bright red "open" sign, Tarel returned to his place behind the counter and waited...

CHAPTER THREE

THE MIRROR OF HIS SOUL

Reece Evans hurried past *Altered States* wishing for the umpteenth time that the *Mystic Market* would move to a better part of town. If they didn't carry the special herbal cleansers and lotions that he used, Reece wouldn't be caught dead in this part of town. As far as he was concerned, only druggies, hoodlums, and other losers frequented the area. It made him nervous to think that there were people who deliberately mutilated their bodies with strange paintings or, even worse, holes that nature hadn't put there. He caught his reflection in the huge glass window sporting pictures of various designs some so-called artist could rip into a customer's skin.   Assorted posters announcing upcoming concerts featuring bands Reece had never heard of and wouldn't go see even if he had, helped hide the clientele of *Altered States* from public view.   He was just as glad he couldn't see anything more than his image in the glassy surface.   Reece had what he liked to call "Superman Black" hair. It was styled impeccably, and had a warm healthy sheen. Penetrating green eyes smiled coldly from a strong tanned face.   Raising a perfectly manicured hand, he straightened his leather jacket. The motion immediately emphasized his broad, well-shaped shoulders. His body was as perfectly manicured as his hands.   *I would never consider marring such a perfect canvas,* he thought. *Even if I did want a tattoo, there isn't a picture worthy of being permanently placed anywhere on me. Unless it was one of me.* Reece smiled to himself. *Not only good lookin', but damn witty, too.* He always could amuse himself, but then Reece often believed that he was his own best company.

Just as he started across the street to the *Mystic Market*, Reece spotted a store he didn't remember seeing the last time he was in Old Towne. His curiosity immediately kicked into gear. The wooden sign that hung in front of the store declared it to be an antique store. He had been looking for extra pieces for his new penthouse apartment, and antiques were not only "in," but could be a good investment. Reece decided to check it out.

As he got closer to the shop, Reece noticed a smaller sign hanging under the one that declared the name of the store. When he got close enough, he could read the small print, and almost walked away. Reece never was one to believe in anything that couldn't be physically examined. Things like wishes were childish. Besides, he firmly believed that he didn't have to wish for things—he just got them. After all, Reece was of the unshakable opinion that nothing could ever be denied him. Anyone who looked like him, dressed like him, and had as much money as he did, didn't need someone else to fulfill anything. It didn't matter that he hadn't earned so much as a penny of the money that he had in fact inherited from his father and grandparents. Everything he had was given to him simply because he deserved it, because he was, after all, the epitome of manly perfection.

Reece shoved the door open and walked into the dimly lit store. It took a few seconds for his eyes to adjust to the sudden change between the bright sunny day filling the outside world and the shadowy realm of the "antique" shop. When the merchandise finally became clear, he noticed that compared to the highly polished items positioned in the windows, everything inside seemed dusty, as if they had been there for a very long time. For some reason, the dust bothered Reece. It wasn't just because he liked things clean, which he did. It was something else. The dust seemed almost too perfect, like it had been added simply to create an atmosphere befitting such a business. He didn't notice the strange old man sitting behind the counter until he spoke. Reece jumped and turned to face the shopkeeper. "May I help you, sir?" The old man's eyes seemed too young and lively for such a crevice-lined face, and his voice was a deep, resonant baritone should have belonged to an opera singer or, at least, a television announcer. He couldn't quite connect it to the grey, wizened antiquarian who had spoken.

The youthful dark eyes peered from a face ravaged by time, the wrinkles embedded deep in his skin. Grey, thinning hair pulled taut across his scalp and into a lank ponytail in back almost covered his liver-spotted head.

Reece blinked as if to clear his vision before responding to the ancient shopkeeper, "I'm just looking," He tried to avoid staring directly at the old man. Anything that old and ugly made him nervous. Reece preferred to be surrounded by beautiful things.

"Are you looking for anything in particular?" The shopkeeper slowly moved from behind the counter.

If the cracked face and stringy gray hair had made Reece uncomfortable, the misshapen body that held up the creature's head made him downright nauseated. To Reece, the shopkeeper's body looked twisted and warped, almost as if he were a caricature of a human being. It dragged one crooked leg a little behind the other, making its entire body seem like the trunk of an old tree that had been twisted and mangled in a terrible storm. Reece fought to keep from screaming, which was something he had never done, and didn't intend on doing now. He caught the urge in his chest and mentally shoved it down. There was no way he wanted to appear as anything less than perfectly calm in front of this *thing*.

Squaring his shoulders, Reece announced in an overly confident voice that he was looking for some accent pieces for a new penthouse apartment in a very exclusive neighborhood so only the best would do. Realizing he was on the verge of babbling, Reece once again reached inside himself and calmed his inner turmoil before continuing: "However, I don't know exactly what I'm looking for; I'll let you know if

I find something." His lighthearted voice sounded forced. Reece didn't like it when he didn't feel in control. There was something about the ancient human standing in front of him that made him feel like running.

The gnarly old man nodded understandingly. "Feel free to look around as much as you wish. I know every piece in this building as well as I would know my own children, if I had any." The look in the old man's eyes made Reece shiver. For some reason, he felt as though the old man had reached into his soul and pulled out a piece for examination. His gaze bore into Reece's brain. He could still feel its intense scrutiny as he turned and walked toward the back of the store.

At first, Reece didn't really notice the objects around him. The dust had caught his eye originally, but he hadn't really examined the contents of the store. After a few moments, he managed to quiet his discomfort, and began to actually look at the wide assortment of merchandise displayed throughout the store. Paintings of every style imaginable hung all over the walls interspersed with signs declaring that the shop offered "Free Delivery on Purchases Over $500." Furniture of all sizes, shapes, and types crowded each other for space, leaving only a narrow aisle for customers to walk through. Every available flat surface held something. There were jewelry, music, and cigar boxes. Figurines of everything imaginable, and some unimaginable things, filled every available nook and cranny. Reece's senses were overwhelmed by the texture, smell, and color of the objects that surrounded him. He saw cases filled with brightly sparkling jewelry. Gowns, capes, suits, and other articles of clothing hung on hooks or special racks that rolled in between various furnishings. The velvets, satins, leathers, and furs were brighter, richer, and softer than any Reece had ever seen. He touched coats that caressed the skin, wrapping the wearer in a cloud of utter luxury. Only later did Reece wonder how so much stuff fit into what was clearly a fairly small store. He turned a corner, stepping around a large, beautifully engraved grandfather clock, and stopped dead. *How perfect* was the first thought that popped into his head.

In front of him was a graceful mirror, over six feet tall and framed in solid oak. As Reece got closer, he noticed a strange design carved into the frame. If his eyes caught it in a certain way, the markings seemed to writhe, twisting into a multitude of combinations as if they were living creatures trying to break from some bizarre wooden prison. Reece blinked, unsure of what he thought he had seen and not willing to admit it even if he had been sure. He refused to dwell on it, because at that moment nothing mattered except getting his hands on that mirror. He had never wanted anything so bad in his life.

He took a step closer. The mirror looked vaguely familiar. He had seen those strange markings somewhere before, but couldn't quite place them. Reece reached out his hand to touch the frame. The room seemed to shake for a split second, and the mirror's surface filled with writhing color. It undulated urgently, then began to slow down almost as though it danced to some strange music Reece couldn't hear. He couldn't tear his eyes away from the clouds of color playing across the surface of the mirror. Reece could feel the wood pulsating warmly beneath his hand. Suddenly, he remembered where he had seen a similar mirror before—hanging in his grandparents' bedroom.

The mirror hadn't been as large as the one standing in front of him, but the wooden frame held the same markings as this one. Reece had been eight years old the last time he remembered seeing it, shortly before his grandparents' death. Memories began rushing back. He had spent a lot of time with his grandparents. They had died in a tragic plane crash on their way to Washington, D.C. Senator David Evans had been on his way back to the nation's capital with his wife and son, Reece's father, to receive an award for all his years of service. Reece's mother, Chloe, had remained behind because she had committed to run some charity function or other. Reece hung on to his memories of his father that his mother didn't know about. He wouldn't share those memories with anyone, especially her. He knew if he did, she would take them away from him somehow. Many of his memories of his father and his grandparents were heavily colored by years of his mother's influence, but not all of them. Some he kept deep within himself.

Jason Evans had just been elected to fill his father's senate seat when the crash occurred. Like his father, Jason truly believed that it was his job to *help* the people. He really wanted to make the world a better place. But Reece didn't remember him as the brilliant, handsome young senator who was on the fast track to the White House. Reece remembered him as the father who played ball with him, the father who sneaked cookies and milk into his room late at night, and the father who tried to answer every question he had as honestly and completely as he could. It was the one thing about his father Reece never let his mother's words touch.

As much as he loved his father, Reece loved his grandparents even more. Whenever his parents had to appear at some charity or political function, Reece would stay with his Grandpa David and Grandma Laura. Grandma Laura would make fresh, buttery popcorn for them to eat while she read him stories.

Reece remembered an incident involving his grandparents' mirror when he was about four. Grandma Laura had tucked him into their bed and settled beside him. When she began reading *Peter Pan* for the third time that week, Reece caught a motion in the mirror out of the corner of his eye. Turning to look directly at the mirror, Reece remembered seeing what appeared to him to be magical images floating within the silver surface. The images seemed to be watching him. He remembered pointing at the mirror and telling his grandmother to "look at Tinkerbell!" At that instant, his grandfather walked in, and the images vanished. From that point, Reece secretly thought of the strangely carved mirror hanging in his grandparent's bedroom as a magic mirror. He had spent hours watching the mirror, waiting for the magic to happen again. It never did. Fearing he was developing an unhealthy obsession, Chloe Evans insisted that Reece be forbidden to stay with his grandparents any longer. Reece remembered that as being the first time he'd ever seen his grandfather on the verge of anger. They compromised by promising to keep their bedroom locked when Reece was there.

Compromise was Senator David Evans' specialty. It was this ability to see both sides of any question that ensured Senator Evans re-election year after year. He had served the state of Missouri for over forty years with most of them spent living in Washington, D.C. Two weeks before Reece's eighth birthday, David Evans decided to retire to spend more time with his wife and grandson, even though he had been begged to run for another term. Reece's grandfather truly believed the platitudes he spouted, as did Reece's father. The son definitely reflected the father. Both cared about the people they represented, and at least tried to always put others before themselves. Reece remembered his grandfather telling him that the only path to true happiness was in the helping of others, and could almost hear his long-dead father reminding him to "treat others as you would like to be treated." When Reece was little, he believed everything his grandfather and father told him. But that all changed after their death. His mother made him see that nobody would help him if he didn't help himself. She told him over and over again that the only people they could trust were each other. She told him her dreams and made them become his dreams, and mom had some big dreams.

Chloe Evans decided she was a princess early on in life. She planned on doing everything she could to make that fantasy a reality. Chloe knew Reece's father was the "one," even before she met him. She married Jason Evans believing that the son would eclipse the father, placing Chloe firmly on the path to the White House. In America, there is no royalty. The closest thing to nobility resided at 1600 Pennsylvania Avenue, and Chloe Evans had every intention of making that her address. The only reason she married Jason was to become the woman behind the President. When Reece's father and grandparents died, Chloe's ambition moved from her husband to her son. For the first time in Reece's life, his mother began paying attention to him. She made sure he wore the right clothes, had the right friends, and attended the right schools. Chloe became even more involved in her charity work as long as it was high profile. She needed to be high profile in order to make as many important contacts as possible. If she couldn't get to the White House, then she was determined that her son would. Chloe Evans had told her son how it was his destiny to be President for so long that even Reece believed it. He knew his mother was manipulating every step he took to achieve her own dream. If she couldn't be First Lady, then she would be First Mother. Either way, Chloe Evans would still be a part of American royalty. Reece didn't care about his mother's dreams, it wouldn't be long until he held all the cards and would tell *her* what to do. Reece wanted the same thing his mother did, but for his own reasons.

Reece pulled away from the mirror, remembering how his mother had called his grandparents' mirror ugly and then promptly sold it, along with most of their possessions, not long after their funerals. He had wanted to keep the mirror, but Reece had known better than to ask his mother to let him have it. Chloe had never really cared for her in-laws, but only tolerated them because she knew their son would follow in his father's footsteps

At that moment, Reece felt the flame of rebellion flare up within him. The undulating colors slowly vanished, and the energy that emanated from the mirror ebbed away. He might regret it later, but he would buy the mirror for his penthouse apartment. Besides he could always use another mirror around the house. He couldn't have too many of those. Reece turned to retrace his steps to the front of the store to make arrangements for the purchase. Reece hadn't taken more than two steps when the storekeeper silently shuffled around the grandfather clock.

"I see you've spotted something that strikes your fancy." The old man's melodious voice seemed tinged with sadness. "This is a very special piece, *very* special. It must be handled carefully." He acted as though he was going to say something else, but had thought better of it. He just shook his head slowly from side to side as if to infer that Reece didn't know what he was doing, which made Reece want the mirror even more.

"How much?" Reece asked firmly, wanting to clearly establish that he was in control of the situation.

The warped body of the shopkeeper stiffened as he hardened his gaze in response to Reece's sharp request. It was clear that he felt reluctant to part with the mirror. A battle seemed to wage within the twisted caricature of a human before he finally sighed and quietly responded with, "The price is $800.00—cash. I do not have the technology to take either credit cards or checks. I only do business in cash."

If this old man thinks that's going to run me off, he's got something else coming, Reece thought as he reached for his wallet. Reece always carried plenty of cash on him. He enjoyed the looks on people's faces as he dropped twenty-dollar tips like confetti at a political rally. He certainly enjoyed the expression on the old geezer's face as Reece removed his platinum and diamond money clip from the back pocket of his jeans, and carefully counted out eight one hundred-dollar bills. Just as he started to hand the money over, Reece noticed a small hand mirror lying on a table near the larger mirror he was about to purchase. It appeared to be made from the same material as the one he wanted, and had smaller versions of the same markings as its larger counterpart, surrounding the frame.

"How much for this small one?" Reece motioned toward the little mirror.

"Consider it a bonus gift," the old man replied as he reached for the cash. Reece spotted the reluctance that caused the shopkeeper's hand to shake, and decided to be magnanimous. A little sweetness, even the artificial kind, can make any transaction go smoother—and quicker.

A vague uneasiness began to creep over Reece. He wasn't exactly afraid, just jittery. Reece didn't like the feeling and if a few false words would get him out the door faster, he was more than willing to use them.

"Look, if it'll make you feel better, I promise to take good care of it. I always take care of everything I own. Remember, your sign promises to grant dreams, and this is the most fantastic mirror I could ever dream of owning, so you have fulfilled your pledge."

The old man snorted with disgust and grabbed the money from Reece's hand. "Young man, I don't need your condescending attitude nor do I need your pity. You should be careful of dreams—some of them can easily turn into nightmares." He reached into the pocket of his apron and pulled out a multi-copy form. "Fill this out and write the directions to where you want the mirror delivered. It will be there by 6:00 p.m. tomorrow evening."

"Can you deliver the smaller mirror to a different address?" Reece asked.

"Wherever you want, just fill out another form with the proper address," the old man pulled off another set of forms and handed them to Reece.

Reece took the papers and wrote out all the information with flourish. He smiled as he filled in Julie's name and address for the smaller mirror. Reece knew Julie liked antiques, and the small mirror looked like it could be even older than the larger one he was purchasing.

Feeling very self-satisfied, he handed back the forms. "Nice doing business with you," he said, his voice dripping with sarcasm. The old man's veiled warning had just made Reece more stubborn. It was as though the old man had insinuated that Reece was in some way inferior. *At least I got the last laugh*, Reece thought as he headed toward the front of the store. He grasped the door handle to open it, and heard the old man's voice softly behind him.

"Don't forget the last part of our motto. That's where the nightmares are born."

Reece whipped around, preparing to firmly tell the ugly old shopkeeper just where he could get off, but the words died in his mouth. The old man was gone and, somehow, the store seemed to be getting smaller, seemed to be slowly shrinking in upon itself. Stumbling over his own feet, Reece ran out the door, almost cracking his head open on the sign hanging from the porch as he leapt for the sidewalk.

Once he was standing in the bright sunshine, he turned

back toward the store, watching as it slowly faded from sight. The last thing he remembered seeing was the sign, and the last words of the store's motto, "...not everything here may be what it seems." Reece felt a ripple of terror course through him. It gripped his body, and he stood frozen, staring at the vacant lot that now stood in place of the antique store. Reece shivered violently, and broke free from his terror-stricken trance. Not even stopping to look for traffic, Reece ran toward his car, hopped in and sped away.

Reece simply drove for a few minutes, trying to gain some sort of composure. He wasn't even positively sure where he was going. For the moment, he didn't care. The longer Reece thought about what had just happened, the surer he became that it was nothing more than an overactive imagination brought on by a combination of the heat of the day, the words of the strange, ugly old man, and the memories of a four year old child. Suddenly, he remembered he had promised to take Julie to dinner tonight. He definitely didn't want Julie to see any weakness. Nothing was ever supposed to mar the perfect image he felt he presented to the world, and especially to Julie. Reece told himself it had to simply be the byproduct of a long day. He would head home, clean up, and get ready for his date with Julie. Being with Julie was an important step in the big picture Reece had envisioned for his life. It helped that his mother agreed with this part of his life plan, even if she didn't know everything.

Reece planned to marry Julie soon. Julie Jeffers was the daughter of one of the senior partners in the law firm Reece had joined after graduating from Harvard. Marrying her would cement the last few links in his chain of power—a chain of power that would lead him to the office that his father would've occupied had he lived. It didn't hurt that Julie was beautiful. Julie's long, always stylish blonde hair complimented the green eyes that intelligently peered from her perfectly symmetrical face. She stood about four inches shorter than Reece, but when Julie wore heels, Reece could stare straight into her eyes. They made a striking couple, and Reece knew it.

Reece forced his clutching fingers to relax on the steering wheel. He couldn't afford to be seen as weak. Weakness would get him killed, just like it got his father and grandparents killed. They didn't have to make the trip in person, but his grandfather told him that they "owed it to the people" to show up. The only thing helping people got them was dead. Reece always remembered that message. He planned on helping himself before helping anybody else.

The drive home took Reece about forty-five minutes. By the time he got there, Reece had thoroughly convinced himself that the vanishing store had just been an illusion. *After all,* he rationalized to himself; *it's a hot day. I probably just had a touch of heatstroke. A person can see all kinds of things if they get too hot.* He knew the store had to have been there. He still had the receipt promising the delivery of the mirror at 6:00 p.m. tomorrow. *I just let that crazy old man's weird comments get to me.* Reece heaved a relieved sigh and smiled to himself. The old man had almost got to him. Deciding to forget about the entire episode, Reece sped up a bit. He didn't want to be late for his date. Reece was always on time—*always*. Besides he didn't want to upset Julie. His and his mother's picture perfect vision of Reece's future relied on his marrying Julie. As far as he was concerned, she had belonged to him even before he proposed to her. That she had said "yes," branded Julie as his property.

Reece had promised Julie's father he would take good care of his little girl. It wasn't a difficult promise for Reece to make. He always took care of his possessions—all of them. Julie's father made sure she had the best education, and her mother made sure she had the right connections. She was intelligent, but seemed caught up in stepping into the stereotypical world inhabited by her own mother. She was already taking her allotted place in society. She belonged to all the right clubs, attended all the right parties, and wore all the right designer clothes. It suddenly occurred to Reece that Julie could be using him in the same way he was using her. What if *she* thought of him as simply a necessary accessory that must be worn to achieve what she wants?

He tried to push the thought away; it made him feel degraded. For a split second, he caught himself wondering how she felt when he treated her like a necessary part of his public persona. Reece was shaken. It hadn't occurred to him to think how other people feel for a very long time. He could almost hear the voices of his father and grandfather whispering to him, telling him all those platitudes he remembered from his short time with them. Do Unto Others. Respect Must Be Earned. Baloney! Reece heard the voice of his mother issuing from his memory. Do Unto Others Before They Do Unto You. Respect Must Be Taken. *Besides I deserve everything I can get...I deserve respect just for being who I am.* Reece grasped onto his mother's words and drew strength from them. He had heard his mother say those exact same words so many times they were engraved into his mind. The important thing was his future, not Julie's. After all, Julie was just a part of the portrait comprising Reece's future. Their future was a work of art that Reece and Chloe Evans were carefully crafting.

Reece felt better the minute he walked into his new penthouse apartment. Even though there were still a lot of packing boxes lying around, Reece felt glad to be home. A hot shower improved his attitude even further. After getting dressed for the evening, Reece paused by the phone. He almost picked it up to give Julie a call to let her know he was on his way. Reece stopped himself. He patted the receiver and walked away, confident once again that he had regained his composure.

Reece pulled up at Julie's apartment building and slipped the doorman a twenty to watch his car while he went up to get her. Glancing at his watch, Reece smiled. *8:00 exactly*, he thought as he walked into the elevator that would take him to Julie's loft apartment.

Julie answered the door wearing a form fitting, black cocktail dress. Her long blonde hair framed her heart shaped face perfectly. The green eyes Reece admired so often peered into his as she gave him a quick kiss hello.

"Are you okay?"

Startled, Reece stepped back from the comfort of Julie's arms. It took him a second to respond. "I'm fine. Why do you ask?"

A look of concern filled Julie's eyes. "I don't know. You just seem different somehow."

Reece didn't know what shocked him the most—the real concern that underscored Julie's words or the fact that it touched him that she cared. He managed to once again push those feelings away. It was something he would have to examine later. Now he had to present the proper image to Julie, but somewhere, deep inside, Reece was getting scared again. He didn't like the feeling. He hadn't liked it earlier in the day, and he definitely didn't like it now.

"Don't be silly. I'm fine. It's just been a long day." Reece grabbed her coat from the back of the couch and wrapped it around Julie's soft shoulders. "We'd better get going before it gets too late. We don't want to miss our reservation time." He hustled her out the door while silently ordering his jangling nerves to settle down.

Throughout the rest of the evening, everything went perfectly as usual. Reece listened as Julie prattled on about the latest happenings within the cream of society, and how hard she was working to make her mother's latest charity fundraiser a huge success. He said all the right things, but his mind really wasn't on what she was saying.

For the first time since he was a small boy, Reece was confused. His mind kept trying to reconstruct the happenings of the day, to try and find some reason for the distracting emotions and thoughts racing through his brain. In his mind, Reece had always been perfect. His mother told him so. Julie told him so. Even his boss and future father-in-law told him so. Right now, Reece didn't feel perfect, and it scared him.

Reece dropped Julie off at her apartment building, after deciding against joining her for their usual nightcap. He told her that he had to be at court early the next morning. Promising to meet her at the same time the next night, Reece kissed Julie goodbye. Leaving her standing at the curb, Reece sped toward home.

As Reece drove away, Julie turned and headed into the building slowly. She knew Reece probably better than he knew himself. Something had shaken him—deeply. Julie had seen Reece coldly angry. She had seen him act absolutely despicable toward others. She knew how easily it came to Reece to get what he wanted out of others. Her friends kept asking her what she saw in him. It was a question Julie couldn't completely answer. Reece Evans intrigued her and repulsed her at the same time. She saw his capacity for cruelty, but she sensed something else—something worth putting up with all his faults.

Julie knew Reece was using her. She didn't care. In her own way, she was using him as well on a number of different levels. Julie wanted to have her own home, wanted to start a family, and, most of all, wanted a chance to be First Lady, for her own reasons. For one, if Reece did become President, he would need someone to guide him. Julie thought, and hoped, she could do that. She sensed the potential Reece had, but sometimes he scared her. He didn't like having anyone tell him what to do. Julie knew that the only way she could influence him was to make him think her ideas were his.

Reece didn't take Julie seriously. He mostly saw her as arm candy. The perfect socialite with all the right family connections to get him where he wanted to be. Julie let him think that. He seemed to forget that Julie had graduated with a Master's Degree in Political Science from Yale. She had ambitions, too. One day Julie hoped to be in the Oval Office herself. Not as First Lady, but as President. Like Reece's father and grandfather, Julie truly thought she could make the world a better place. She believed that it just might be possible for her to follow Reece into the White House. This dream was a private one for now. Julie had no intention of telling Reece her own ambitions until she was good and ready. Until that day, Julie knew she had to play the game, and Reece was an important part of her strategy.

Julie wanted to help Reece for a number of reasons, for herself and for those his actions would impact if he did make it to the White House, but the biggest one—the one she really didn't understand—was simply that she loved him. That's why she was so worried about him now. Clearly, Reece had not been with Julie tonight. Physically, yes. Mentally, no. On one hand, Reece's actions tonight scared her. On the other hand, Julie felt oddly excited. For once, he had exhibited a hint of weakness in his armor of perfection. As she got out of her clothes and crawled into bed, Julie thought about her future with Reece. She was fully aware of what he and his mother had planned. Neither were exactly quiet about their plans for the future. Julie planned on being a part of those plans even if it she didn't become the first female President. If she could do nothing else, she would do her best to help Reece make the right choices for the right reasons. She knew it might be an impossible task, but it was something she needed to attempt—for herself, for everyone. Reaching over to turn out the bedside lamp, Julie hoped Reece would some day trust her as much as he at least appeared to trust his mother—a misplaced trust as far as Julie was concerned. Turning over in an attempt to get comfortable, Julie wondered once again if Reece truly bought the load of bull his mother continually spouted. She knew Reece well enough to know he was entirely capable of only appearing to be the completely devoted son Chloe Evans thought she had created. As she drifted off to sleep, Julie hoped Reece was getting some rest as well. He had seemed tired and a bit troubled tonight. She knew his mind had not been entirely with her.

Reece was unusually drained. After leaving Julie, Reece went home and fell straight into bed, where he slept hard and deep. The next morning he awakened refreshed and ready to tackle the world. The incidents and emotions of the day before seemed nothing more than a vaguely remembered bad dream. He felt his confidence rising as he took a long, hot shower and got dressed for work.

Reece loved his job. He truly enjoyed handling the details of people's lives. Reece knew the law inside and out. He knew the loopholes just as well. There was never any hint of illegality in Reece's legal maneuverings, but that didn't mean everything he did was strictly legal either. He knew how to manipulate the law to fit almost any client's needs. Usually he could talk people into the outcome he wanted, but if push came to shove, Reece also knew how to do that. He could shove with the best of them. That was one reason why he was considered one of the most promising young lawyers in the field. As a result, Reece made lots of money for the firm as well as for himself. It would just be a matter of time before he made partner. Reece could almost see the plush office that would soon be his. But he didn't plan on stopping there, that's for certain. Reece envisioned his current job as simply a stepping-stone into politics.

He smiled, imagining himself sitting in the Oval Office, as he left work after a full day of satisfying legal machinations. He unlocked the front door to his penthouse and walked into the living room. Putting down his leather briefcase, Reece stretched, releasing the tension in his neck, shoulders, and arms that came from spending hours sitting in front of the computer or on the telephone. He was tired, but self-satisfied. It had been a good day—a very good day. Four new clients and two wins in State Court were nothing to sneeze at. His boss was duly impressed. Mr. Jeffers had even hinted that the larger office Reece felt he deserved would soon be his. Yes. It had been a *very* good day. The doorbell buzzed, breaking into Reece's smug fantasy. At first, he was annoyed. Being interrupted was irritating, especially when he could better spend the time thinking about his favorite subject— himself.

Opening the door, Reece was immediately confronted with a very large shipping box and an ordinary looking man in uniform.

"Mr. Evans?"

"I'm Reece Evans."

"I've got a package for you. Sign here." The deliveryman handed Reece a computer-linked pad, showing him where to write his name with a special pen that would electronically verify his receipt of the package.

Reece signed and before he could even open his mouth to ask a question, the deliveryman turned and walked away abruptly. Reece was no longer simply annoyed. Mad barely covered the emotion raging through him. He quickly followed the deliveryman.

"Hey! Where do you think you're going?" Reece yelled. "Stop!"

Reece couldn't believe it. The man acted like he didn't even hear Reece. He simply walked purposefully down the hall, pausing only to make a right turn through a door into the delivery elevator area. Reece was no more than three or four steps behind the deliveryman, but when he made that same turn—no one was there. The weirdest part of the whole thing was that Reece didn't hear the delivery elevator running. Usually the thing made so much noise the entire building sounded like it was ready to lift off its foundation and head for outer space. There was no other way out, so he had to have taken the elevator. Reece smiled sardonically. A part of him knew he was rationalizing the situation, but he didn't care. As long as he was right, and he always was, nothing else mattered. He definitely was not going to go running after some lazy deliveryman. Reece would call the company and make sure that the man would never delivery anything, anywhere, ever again.

"The least he could've done is help me move it in the house," Reece muttered to himself as he walked back down the hall and wrestled the oversized package into his living room. After going into the kitchen and fetching an exacto knife from the tool drawer, he sliced open the box. The first thing visible was an abundance of packing material. Pulling apart the box and leaving styrofoam popcorn scattered across the room like hail after a major thunderstorm, he slowly revealed the mirror he had purchased from the crazy old man the day before.

At first, he couldn't believe it. He had managed to push the events of the previous day out of his mind, but the appearance of the mirror brought everything back in a rush. Reece couldn't deny that at least part of yesterday's occurrences had a basis in reality and not completely in the effects of the day's heat. The mirror standing in front of him was real, tangible proof that the store had actually been there. He shook himself and pulled away from the sinister path his mind wanted to take. He couldn't be going crazy. *It had to be the heat. Going from the heat, into the coolness of the store, and back out into the heat had to have been why I saw what I thought I saw,* Reece rationalized to himself, *If I drove back to Old Towne, the store would be there.* Reece smirked, glancing around the empty room thankful that no one was around to see his uncertainty. Reece wouldn't or couldn't admit, even to himself, that he was anything less than the best in whatever it was—his looks, his possessions, and most of all, his control of any and every situation. But something about the mirror spooked him. It caused him to struggle with feelings he thought he had managed to bury when his father and grandparents died. Now it stood before him.

Pulling away the rest of the packing material, Reece completely revealed the full-length mirror. Its elegant design and graceful form struck him once again. Checking out his reflection in its highly polished surface, Reece couldn't help stopping to admire his own handsome exterior. His inner turmoil subsided as he took in the broad shoulders and precisely proportioned torso which complimented his strong, muscled legs and well-shaped hips. Reece really did enjoy looking at himself. *Not bad at all,* Reece thought as he checked himself out. *Now, I've got a mirror that truly reveals my good side.* He gave a slow turn. *But then again, I don't have anything but good sides. I just keep getting better looking every day.* There was something about standing in front of this mirror that made Reece feel like really examining himself. Staring blindly into the mirror, Reece removed his clothes without even noticing. He fixated on his own body—its texture, its intricate shadings of color and its graduating muscles. Reece continued to admire himself for what seemed to him only a few minutes. He probably would've gone on even longer if the telephone hadn't rung. Expecting a phone call from his boss and irritated because he knew he had to answer it, he jerked up the receiver and growled, "Hello," before catching himself. A small finger of shock traveled up his spine. Reece never lost control like that. He had used the same nasty tone deliberately before, but this was the first time he had let his emotions take over his mouth. He felt even more irritated when the voice on the other end was Julie's.

"Hi, Reece. You told me that you were coming by to get me for dinner at 8:00. It's almost 9:30, are you okay?" The concern in her voice sounded real. She knew that he would never be late unless something had happened. He was way too punctual.

After hearing her tone, Reece wondered what Julie saw in him. He felt another trickle of fear. The concept of wondering what other people thought of him hadn't occurred to Reece. Not since his father and grandparents died. He shoved that notion as far away as he could by reminding himself how great he was, which, of course, Julie knew. *Sure, she was concerned, why shouldn't she be? She's lucky to have me. Hell, I'm too good for her. I only need her for her connections. She's going to help me get where I want to go. Then everyone will understand and appreciate me, and the power I will hold. If they don't, then they'll pay.* But something about those thoughts felt wrong to Reece. Reece felt his overpowering self-confidence begin to fade. He did the only thing he could think of. Reece got *angry.* All of a sudden, Reece didn't want anything to do with Julie. She was beneath him. He could find someone better, someone more suited to the role as mate of the handsomest and, soon to be, most powerful man in the world.

"I got busy. You know I have things to do, *important* things." Reece let his newly discovered disgust toward Julie shine through his words. "I'll call you tomorrow."

"Are you sure you're okay?"

"Don't question me! I hate it when people question my decisions. I said I'd call you tomorrow." Reece voice shook with ill-concealed rage.

"I'll talk to you tomorrow then," Julie said softly, a hint of tears leaking into her voice.

Slamming down the receiver, Reece started to pull the cord from the wall. He had always hated it when people questioned him about his business. His mother was the only person he had ever allowed to question his decisions, and sometimes he even resented her. Just then the tears in Julie's voice came back to him. For a split second, he almost picked up the receiver to call her back and apologize. But he could hear his mother's voice reminding him that he didn't have to be sorry for anything. It occurred to Reece that he had violated his own prime directive. He had shown weakness. That thought made him even angrier. Reece jerked the cord with so much strength, he pulled the face plate off the wall along with the cord, ensuring there would be no more interruptions to his saturation in the well of self-absorption threatening to drown him.

Reece knew he would figure out something to tell Julie tomorrow. Something she would buy. She always did. He needed to keep her on a string in case he couldn't find someone more appropriate for the exalted position of First Lady. Reece had to keep thinking of Julie in those terms. It was his future that was important—he would do whatever it took to ensure he fulfilled his destiny. He would worry about Julie tomorrow. For tonight, just for tonight, Reece wanted to put his future on hold. For now, Reece wanted to thoroughly examine the mirror. He seemed drawn to it in a way that both comforted and frightened him.

Reece turned back toward the mirror, catching the clock on the VCR out of the corner of his eye. *9:30 p.m.* It really was 9:30! The mirror had been delivered at six and, as far as he was concerned, it had been no more than ten or fifteen minutes between that time and Julie's phone call. Yet, if the clock was right, then he had lost several hours. The fear that had begun earlier as a trickle, now began to widen into a growing flood.

After Reece hung up on her, Julie stared in growing horror at the telephone hanging limply in her hand. She almost rushed over to his penthouse, but stopped herself before she even fully completed the thought. Walking over to the mantle, Julie picked up the small wooden handled mirror that had been delivered that afternoon. Although there was no card attached, Julie assumed it was a present from Reece. After their phone conversation, Julie wasn't so sure Reece had sent it. She stared at the exotic markings embedded in the wood. They seemed to glow with a strange energy that soothed her nerves and eased the ache around her heart. It almost seemed to talk to her. Suddenly she knew why she couldn't go to Reece—the time was not right. Julie knew that in order to save him, she had to let Reece Evans go. It was his journey, not hers. She gently laid the mirror down and walked into the other room.

Fear controlled Reece's muscles. He was frozen in place, trapped by his own image being reflected back into his wide eyes from the shifting, silvery surface of the mirror. *What the hell is going on here?* Reece thought, trying to force his feet to put distance between himself and the now vaguely threatening reflection. There was no reason to fear his own image, but he did. He could feel his own eyes drawing him into a whirling cloud of images and words that overwhelmed him. Reece wished he hadn't torn the phone from the wall, but then he wouldn't have been able to walk over to it even if he hadn't trashed the phone. He wanted to call Julie more than anything at that moment. The thought vaguely surprised him. He hadn't thought of calling his mother, but Julie. Looking around the room, Reece spotted his leather briefcase and could see the bulge of his cell phone in its compartment. *My cell phone. Maybe I can reach my cell phone.* Trying harder to pull himself out of the paralysis that held him, Reece only managed to be drawn closer to the mirror. Some part of him had known when he tried it that he wouldn't make it. Tearing the phone out of the wall made no difference. Even if he hadn't, he wouldn't have been able to reach it. Reece remembered the stories his Grandma Laura used to tell him and wondered if he was caught inside one of them.

A vortex of sight and sound encircled him. Reece saw himself through his own eyes as well as those of others. He saw his grandfather and father both reaching out to him. His grandmother floated behind them with a disapproving look on her face as she stared at Reece. Julie's tear-filled eyes confronted him again and again, peering out from the small mirror Reece had sent to her. He wanted to reach out to her, and tell her to throw it away before she became as trapped as he was, but he couldn't speak or move. Reece heard the harsh and sometimes hateful words he spat at people; felt what they were feeling when he talked down to those he felt were beneath him or those he praised with false worship.

Even when he presented his good face, it was a false one veiled in self-promotion, arrogance, and conceit. Over it all, he could see his mother's shadowy figure trying to push past his memories. Her voice reverberated in his skull, telling him, "Don't be weak. Presidents aren't weak. Think of yourself. Think of me. We're the only two that count." He could almost physically feel the cold slickness of her spirit as it fought its way through the warm, comforting voices of his grandparents and his father, trying to bury all the other voices as she had Reece's entire life.

Fighting against visions he could not nor would not believe, Reece's anger and fear could be contained no longer. He did the only thing he could do at this point. He screamed. Deep inside him a kernel of humanity that had been buried, floated free. It would take time for it to be fully born, but it was already pushing forth questing tendrils that Reece could not yet feel. On the verge of losing his sanity, Reece grabbed onto the only thing he had complete confidence in—his vision of himself. He did the one thing he could think of, reaching out toward his own image; Reece could feel the paralysis lift as he fell through the mirror onto the floor.

At first, he was afraid to move, fearing that he would discover his perfect body damaged, or even worse, scarred in some hideous way. He needed his beauty to pave the way to his future. Carefully he shifted first one leg and then the other. They moved, but somehow they didn't feel quite right. It was almost as though they didn't belong to his body. Reece looked down and froze. His lower limbs were twisted, misshapen sticks stretched out below him. When he raised his arm, he saw deep lines covering his hands and vanishing up the sleeve of a plain brown work shirt. An apron covered his pants and also served to keep the wrinkled trousers from falling off his bony hips. Managing to get up on his hands and knees, Reece crawled over to the mirror, which amazingly still stood intact. *This has to be a bad dream, it has to!* He held onto that thought as he pulled himself erect and stared into the reflective surface of the mirror, and saw—himself! His perfect body lay motionless on the floor of his living room. It was at that moment that Reece realized he was no longer at home, but somewhere else entirely.

There was furniture and glassware, jewelry and clothing. Every nook and cranny of the room Reece appeared in was filled with something. He immediately recognized his location. Reece was in that crazy old man's store. Catching his reflection in the glass of a nearby china cabinet, he jumped. That old man was standing right where Reece was standing. He was afraid to look into the mirror that had brought him here, so he carefully approached the sparkling, shiny glass covering the front of the dusty display cabinet. The old man's eyes stared back at him; fear flickering in their depths as he slowly took in the deep wrinkles that creased his face and the wisps of lank gray hair crowning his head. The room seemed to spin crazily as the awareness of his new identity fell upon him. He *was* the gnarly old man.

"Reece..." A familiar voice broke through the waves of sheer terror that washed over him, pulling him back to consciousness away from the insanity filled pit threatening to engulf him. "Reece!" He turned around and stared at the mirror. His own body was staring back at him, but the presence behind the eyes wasn't his. The gnarly old man had taken his place. The hideous, mutilated creature that had sold him the mirror possessed his spectacular body.

"W-w-why, just tell-l-l me why?" Reece finally stuttered

out loud, forcing his lungs to expel the words.

From the handsome face Reece was familiar with, the old man's eyes looked at him with pity. The only thing Reece didn't recognize was the compassion emanating from his own face—a face he no longer wore.

"You have been tried, judged, and convicted. I'm sorry. It wasn't my choice. I was just doing my job."

"Tried...convicted, of what?"

"If you had remained on the path you were treading, the results would have been disastrous. You would have been responsible for the deaths of millions, all because you were so full of yourself that you could never admit a mistake, let alone believe that any kind of imperfection could exist in the fantasy world you wove around yourself."

Reece couldn't believe what he was hearing. "Don't I even get a chance to defend myself? What about justice?"

The now young man laughed. "Justice. You want justice. You were given every chance to defend yourself. The mirror showed you how you treated everyone around you and how he or she felt about that treatment. All you had to do was feel some kind of pity, some kind of compassion, but you couldn't or wouldn't."

"But I was just doing what my mother wanted. Isn't that worth something?" Reece begged.

Tarel snorted in disgust. "Parents shape their children, but, sooner or later, you must take responsibility for yourself. You also had good examples you could have chosen to follow. Why didn't you embrace the teachings of your grandparents, your father, or even Julie? She really cares about you, but for the life of me, I don't know why. The Klebba probably know. They know everything. There were a couple of times I thought you would be one of the lucky ones, but the only thing you were willing to embrace was your own selfishness. Even now you're trying to pass the buck for your own actions. You are one of the forks in the river of history. I know you don't understand now. I couldn't in the beginning, but now the possibilities—the possibilities are endless. Look deep, see what would have happened if you were allowed to continue. Not all possibilities are good. They can be. It just depends on the choices. Look what happens when you make the wrong choice. Look, look...."

His voice slowly faded as a fog seemed to roll across the mirror's surface, twisting, bulging, and writhing with flashes of bright light cutting paths through the gray, almost-living mass. The light grew brighter, pushing aside the fog and revealing a clear summer day. The picture solidified in creeping sections, finally forming the picture of an elegantly appointed office, the place he had dreamed of occupying for years. An older, dignified version of Reece Evans stood with his hands behind his back staring out a window that was letting in the summer light. This was how he would look in the future, if he could find a way to regain control of his body. A door to the right of the future Reece Evans opened up, and a slim, young man in a precisely tailored suit entered.

"Mr. President. You need to get underground. We've only got a couple of minutes until the first missiles impact."

"What does it matter? It's all over now anyway. Why didn't they listen to me? Why did they make me do this? I didn't start this. THEY did. They lost every right they had when they took out the World Trade Center and the Pentagon. Their rights died when that plane hit the ground in Pennsylvania. Everyone knows the Iraqi were helping bin Laden. I had every right to those oil fields. It was compensation for all the pain and suffering this country has gone through. Besides, we needed the fuel. We HAD to have the fuel."

The young man snorted, "Excuse me, sir, but you could have had all the oil you wanted if you hadn't lost your temper and ordered the military to nuke Iraq. By the end of the Afghan operation, they would have given us almost anything we wanted. You doomed us the day you convinced Congress that only you could adequately decide to push the button. *You* put the potential for total destruction in the hands of one irresponsible man, yourself! And when you didn't get what you wanted, the way you wanted it, you pushed the button. Hell, don't go underground. You're right. What difference does it make? We did it to ourselves. We voted for an egotistical, self-involved monster like you. Now we're reaping what we sowed. May God have pity on all our souls!"

The President never moved as the young man left the room, slamming the door on his way out. As a bright light filled the room, evaporating everything it touched, Reece heard the man he could have become sadly announce, "I'm going to miss being me." The regal figure vanished in a blast of fire and energy, filling the mirror with brightness so glaring, Reece had to turn away and cover his eyes.

His own voice confronted him once again. "This is what you are capable of, and why you had to be removed. You will take my place, travelling from world to world and sometimes back, finding those whose existence has the potential to destroy not only their own worlds, but could have a terrible impact upon others. This is your punishment for the crime you would have committed. You have no choice, just like I had no choice."

"What about me...er...you?" Reece choked out, trying to maintain at least a semblance of composure.

"Me?" The man inhabiting the body he once had the pleasure of occupying stretched his powerful muscles. "I'm going to enjoy not hurting every time I move, that's for sure. But you better take care of that old body you are wearing now. It's special to me. I'm just taking yours on loan. You do have the possibility of winning it back, but you have to learn not to care about it first." Tarel shook his head. "You don't understand yet. You simply don't know how. But one day you will and then you'll really understand how this world has the potential to transform the galaxy in ways not even I can imagine. It carries the seeds of hope as well as the potential for great destruction. What happens here can affect thousands of worlds in countless galaxies. It's the Klebba's job to help those who aren't mature enough yet to help themselves. I see them as the gardeners of the universe cutting out weeds trying to choke the galaxy."

"They sound a little too goody two-shoes to me." Reece snorted.

Tarel shook his head. "You don't know the meaning of good and evil yet, but you will, and you'll learn."

"Or what?" Reece asked.

Tarel shrugged. "That's up to fate and, of course, the Klebba."

"The Klebba?" Reece asked. "Just who is this Klebba person you keep talking about?"

"Not a Klebba, *the* Klebba. Don't worry about them yet. They'll let you know what you need to know, when and only when you need to know it. I've learned, just like you'll learn, not to ask too many questions. You'll find out who they are and what they do when *they* decide the time is right. If you ever want to get out of that rotting hulk of a body, you'll have to do some serious soul searching and let me tell you one thing for sure—looking deep in your own soul and contemplating what lives there will be ten times more difficult than seeing yourself in a mirror, even in that body. If you're lucky, *really lucky*, you just might be able to reclaim your life. It's ultimately up to you."

With that final awful warning, the image of the body he had worn for so long faded away, leaving Reece standing alone in the middle of a store that wasn't a store, moving toward a future he couldn't even conceive. He was alone with only himself. Reece wasn't sure he liked it, but he had no choice. There was nowhere to run, nowhere to hide. He could only stand there and wait for his sentence to begin.

A strange energy flowed over Reece's body. His skin felt as if it were covered with millions of ants scurrying for cover. His stomach tried to crawl up his throat toward freedom. Sliding into the peaceful darkness of his own mind, Reece fainted.

CHAPTER FOUR

THE JOURNEY BEGINS

As the blackness lightened toward gray, Reece heard a soft, hissing voice calling to him. "Rees-s-s, it's-s-s time to wake up." He rolled over; vaguely wishing his nanny would let him sleep in just once, school or no school.

"Rees-s-s, we don't have much time. You mus-s-st wake up." The voice was a little louder this time.

Reece tried to ignore the voice. He didn't want to wake up yet. Rolling over, he blindly searched for the blanket to pull over his head.

"Rees-s-s!"

He woke with a start still reaching for a blanket that wasn't there. Jerked from the comforting dream of his mother's presence—of her stroking his hair and telling him over and over again just how perfect he was, Reece was confronted by a vision that threatened to immediately force his mind to return to the safety of oblivion. Standing before him was a being of indescribable beauty. At first, Reece thought he was dead, and this being standing in front of him was an angel. He, she, it—Reece wasn't sure which gender it fell into, or even if it had any kind of gender at all. The creature had a humanoid shape. Reece could see two long arms and two lean, muscled legs. The hairless head as well as the rest of the being's slender body seemed surrounded in some kind of energy shield. He couldn't make out any specific features. The shifting colors of the field surrounding the creature moved smoothly as it raised its arms. The glowing being revealed delicate hands with long fingers that were also encased in the shield.

"I am not armed. I will not hurt you." The alien angel's voice seemed caring, yet Reece caught the undertones that told him not to mess with his visitor. It might appear like an angel, but could quickly turn into something Reece didn't have the nerve to deal with, not now, not after what he'd been through. It slowly lowered its arms.

"Tarel has informed you of your s-s-sentence." The words were *not* a question, but a firm statement of fact.

Reece could feel anger building within him once again. He had just about had enough. "What crime? You're convicting me for something I haven't done yet. You have no..."

"Enough!" The creature cut him off in mid-sentence. "If we do not s-s-stop you, then countles-s-s millions-s-s will die. Not jus-s-st your mother or Julie, but your entire planet will be s-s-scrubbed cleaner than the vacuum of s-s-space. Even with that, we would not have interfered, but the repercus-s-sions-s-s from what you began would have been dis-s-sas-s-strous-s-s for the entire galaxy. We have obs-s-served your people for a long time. When you walked into the s-s-shop, you reached a fork in the road of time. It brought you to this-s-s point in his-s-story." It bent closer to him, pity and more than a bit of sadness seemed to influence the colors in the field as it became predominately blue. "You are definitely not a prime example of your s-s-species-s-s, but your people do have great potential. One that mus-s-st be allowed to grow and expand. When the time comes-s-s and the people of the Earth have reached their full growth, when they have come of age, then their actions-s-s, their vis-s-s-ions-s-s, their wis-s-sdom will join together a multitude of worlds-s-s. If Earth and her people can s-s-survive their adoles-s-scence, then maybe, s-s-someday, they will join with ours-s-s in the greates-s-st adventure of them all—the journey toward the next level of exis-s-stence."

The first thing Reece thought after the creature finished speaking was *What a load of bull!* Just as he started to launch a spectacular tirade at the glowing vision standing in front of him, the being sighed with disgust. The hissing voice suddenly became clearer, firmer. "I knew it was-s-s too s-s-soon to believe you had even caught a glimmer of what I am attempting to s-s-say. Contemplate the images-s-s in the mirror, the ones-s-s that called from the depths-s-s of your s-s-soul. Think about your father, your grandparents-s-s. *Learn from them.* Only within yours-s-self can you find the path to regaining what you could have been—what you mus-s-s-t become. When you have done that, then you have a chance. Prove you are worthy. Find yours-s-self by helping others-s-s. That is-s your s-s-sentence for your potential, but you *do* have a choice."

"And that is...? Reece asked, already knowing he wouldn't like the response.

"We would have to remove you from this exis-s-stence all together, but the choice is-s-s yours-s-s. Either help us-s-s, help others-s-s, or your exis-s-stence ends-s-s here." The creature seemed sad, as if truly hoping that Reece wouldn't choose that route.

Reece was stunned. He heard but he didn't hear the voice as it told him of the many times and places he would visit. He gathered that he was expected to help others, whether they wanted his help or not, and that in the process he would be helping himself. He learned he would be expected to wear any number of bodies, both human and alien. The thought of being in a body even more grotesque than the one he now wore shook Reece to his very core. For the first time in his life, he was in a situation he couldn't sweet talk or argue his way through. He could feel his confidence ebbing away.

"I don't want to die," Reece whispered. "I'll do whatever you want."

Once again, the being raised its arms, but this time, instead of simply showing empty hands, a warm, blue light emanated from them and enveloped Reece. His mind whirled as if attempting to reject the sensations that filled him. He tried to deny what was being shown him, but he couldn't. Reece remembered the quiet conversations between his father and grandfather as they discussed ways to make the world a better place. He felt his grandmother's love as she told him stories of good people doing great things. He heard Julie's voice, full of concern and love, as she reassured him that he was not alone. His mother's voice and his own ego were silent, and the seed that the Klebba uncovered began to strengthen and grow. It was at this moment that Reece knew why that strange, glowing angel had done this to him. The Klebba cared. Not just about him, but about everyone and everything. It was what they were, and, even more importantly, it was *who* they were.

With the warm, blue light caressing his spirit, Reece felt as though he was no longer alone. Someone cared about what happened to him because they *cared;* not because they thought he was good looking or wealthy or even because they feared him. Now that he thought about it, almost everyone he had known his entire life had wanted something from him. In school, everyone wanted to be his friend because he had money to burn. Girls flocked around him, not because they actually liked him, but because he looked good and ran with the "right" crowd. His mother gave him everything he asked for, but put him on display like a prized possession whenever anybody was around. Reece suddenly realized that the one person left who did love him, Julie, he had thrown away when he had torn the phone from the wall.

The images from the mirror began swarming around him, shifting in and out of the rainbow hued mass of energy embodied within it. One section of twisting color began to solidify. As it gained structure, Reece realized it was his father's worry-lined face confronting him. "Don't listen to your mother, Reece. Follow your heart, son. I know you have a good one if you just set it free."

Reece stretched out his arms, aching to touch his father again. Jason Evans faded into the mass of swirling colors. Taking its place was the strong, firm chinned face of his grandfather. "Reece, you have it in you to help so many people. That's the point of being human. We all should help each other. I know it's cliché, but that doesn't make it less true."

Reece was confused. He didn't know who or what to believe. He didn't know *how* to help anyone else. Right now, Reece couldn't even help himself. He shrank from the image of his grandfather floating before him. He was disgusted with himself. His grandfather's face slid into the colored chaos, only to be replaced by the one person he didn't want to see— his own mother. Reece saw the hard anger burning in her ice blue eyes as she began berating him.

"Snap out of it, Reece. Be a real man. Don't listen to those idiots. They died because they put others first. Your own father cared more about other people than he did you. Don't destroy your future—*my* future. I always said you were perfect. I guess I was wrong." Chloe Evans began laughing. "You won't change. You can't change any more than I can. You're doomed to be what your mother made you—a selfish, egotistical, lonely old man."

Reece could feel anger growing in him once again. This was a different kind of anger. For once, Reece was angry with himself. He couldn't even blame his mother for not teaching him to be more like his father and grandfather. Reece blamed himself. He believed in his mother even when his heart told him not to. Even if he regained his body, Reece would never look at himself in the same way again. Digging below his perfect exterior had revealed a Reece that even he didn't like. Finding a strength he never knew he had, Reece did the one thing he never imagined doing. He stood up to his mother.

"Just shut up. I think you've finally said enough." The look on his mother's face was priceless. He had never seen her at a loss for words before. Chloe Evans image dissolved back into the swirling mass of colors still wearing an expression of shock and disbelief. He had a long way to go, but Reece Evans was on his way to becoming something he had never been before—human.

The light slowly died away, leaving Reece a little empty. He lost a piece of himself in that light, but he didn't think he would miss what had been taken away. Reece felt almost reborn, but a small part of him, a part that wouldn't let go, still whispered to him, warning him to think only of himself.

"You have a long way to go, but the journey has-s-s begun." The creature's sibilant voice penetrated Reece's confused thoughts. "There is-s-s hope for you yet, Rees-s-s Evans-s-s."

Reece was still very confused. "Journey. We're going on a trip."

The glowing being smiled gently at him. "For you, a very long trip on a number of different levels. This-s-s place...this-s-s s-s-ship can take you any place or time. It adapts-s-s its-s-s appearance and its-s-s contents-s-s to fit into any environment, any being, or any culture needed to accomplis-s-sh the des-s-signated miss-s-sion. It may als-s-s-o change you, but only in ways-s-s which will allow you to do what you need to do. The bas-s-sic s-s-shape you now wear will be retained whenever you are on board this-s-s vehicle."

"Change? How?" Reece's wasn't sure he liked the idea of solid objects, especially objects like himself, that could just transform into something else.

The shimmering being regarded Reece indulgently, making him feel like a small child who couldn't understand the question, let alone the answer. The sibilant voice smoothed out as the creature carefully explained to Reece some of the Klebba's history. "The technology behind all of this," it motioned around the room with a very human-like movement of his arm, its voice becoming even more clear, "is beyond your understanding. It took my people thousands of years to develop and perfect it. We almost destroyed our entire civilization because of it. When we discovered that through this technology we could move not only through space, but time, my ancestors realized that they could ensure that our people would survive. It was only later that we realized that once we began the process, we would be forced to expand our horizons beyond our own small world into a galaxy of which we were but a very small part. We discovered that everything is connected—past, present, future. Time flows like a river with many possible branches, some mixing into quiet pools or churning torrents, before branching off yet again. Events on one planet can and do have repercussions in places that you could never imagine. Our people are now ready to expand our horizons even further, to travel on toward the next level of existence, whatever that may be. But we cannot, not yet." It paused as if wondering what to say next.

Reece started to ask another question, but there were too many raging through his crowded mind to express just one. He stared around the room looking for something solid to focus on. Reece noticed that all of the merchandise that had once filled the store was gone. In the place of the assorted pieces of dusty furniture, clothing, and other bric-a-brac were containers of all shapes and sizes. Each storage unit appeared to be made from the same substance as the mirror. He saw his own image reflected hundreds of times in the highly polished surfaces. The same pulsating, multi-hued energy field that inhabited the mirror surrounded Reece. It hovered around him like a rainbow aura. Forcing himself to look again at the being Tarel called a Klebba, Reece remembered Tarel telling him not to ask too many questions. He was beginning to learn patience.

The creature glowed brighter. "You have a long journey ahead. There are other worlds that are perched on the edge of destruction. There are other beings who, like you, need someone to show them the way. Still others have found the proper path, but are blocked by those who cannot or will not see beyond their own desires. Through helping others, we hope that you, too, will learn. Maybe someday, you'll even learn enough to return to your own world."

A flicker of hope sprang up inside Reece. It was different than anything he had
ever felt before. "I'm willing to try. I'll do anything I can to get back to where I was."

The being shook his hairless head sadly as it responded with the same hissing quality that had infected its speech earlier. "Clearly, Reece Evans-s-s has a lot left to learn. S-s-

someday you will have to be able to s-s-see it is-s-sn't where
s-s-someone was-s-s that is-s-s s-s-so important. It is-s-s
where they will be. His-s-story s-s-should be left behind.
What everyone mus-s-st do is focus-s-s on their future his-s-
story. That's-s-s what counts-s-s."

Reece didn't completely understand what the Klebba
was attempting to tell him. He didn't have the strength to try
to comprehend. Once again, Reece could hear his mother
telling him not to listen. With effort, Reece was able to push
his mother's nagging voice behind the mirrored walls of his
mind. He followed its lingering notes, where Reece was forced
to really look at himself again. He didn't want to. A part of
him wanted to clamp his eyes shut and flee screaming into
the safe darkness of his own mind. What he saw made him
cringe in self-disgust, but beneath it all he caught a glimpse
of what he could be. That's what scared him the most. He
wasn't sure he had the kind of courage it was going to take to
reach the potential everyone seemed to think he possessed.
Reece truly realized he was far from perfect. He couldn't
deny the fact. It stared at him through the colored chaos.
His own past, his possible futures, both good and terrifying
played out in the shimmering surface undulating before him.

Shining with an almost unbearable brightness, the
creature's soothing voice pulled Reece from the mind mirror
that held him. "Trying is-s-s only the firs-s-st s-s-step, but it
is-s-s a good one. Be well, Reece Evans-s-s. Now your true
adventure begins-s-s." With those final words, the creature
faded from sight.

Reece stared as the last trails of glowing light faded
into the tall wooden curio cabinet in front of him. Gradually
he realized that the shop had returned. He couldn't begin to
figure out why. Perhaps to make him more comfortable. He
opened the cabinet's mirrored doors and saw nothing but
empty, dust-covered shelves. Reece walked to the front of
the shop until he saw the view outside the store's windows.
The shop was travelling through the velvet blackness of space,
above a bridge of scintillating stars that exhibited every
possible color nature had in her pocket. It was a stream – a

bridge of stars reaching to another place, another time, another *world*. Reece wondered what waited for him out there. He knew he had a long battle ahead. Sensing his mother's presence fighting to gain enough strength to influence him again, Reece pictured Julie in his mind. Combining his strength with memories of Julie, Reece pushed his mother's influence even further away. But he couldn't erase it entirely, not yet. It was too much a part of him.

Reece stared at the stars streaming by and wondered if he would ever reach the potential the Klebba claimed he had. It would be a strange journey. Of that Reece was sure. He only hoped that along the way he would find himself, and in the process, the way home.

CHAPTER FIVE
EARTHBOUND

Tarel moved back away from the mirror and sat on the black leather sofa that dominated Reece's living room. He always felt somewhat nauseated after translocation, whether it involved a body switch or not. When a body switch was added, the nausea was even worse. He not only took on Reece's body, but his memories were implanted into Tarel's mind as well. What Tarel saw there made his stomach churn even harder. Not because he had never experienced anything like Reece's mind, but because it was all too familiar. Tarel knew too well how it felt to be so self-important, so self-absorbed that the destruction of entire star systems didn't even phase him. Tarel knew it because it was like looking into the mind of the man he, himself, had once been.

As the nausea finally began to subside, Tarel took stock of the body he now wore. The ability to stretch his limbs out straight was marvelous. While he could appreciate his new body's strength and good looks, it was the ability to move gracefully and painlessly that Tarel appreciated the most. Still, he preferred the gnarly, pain-ridden body Reece now wore. Wearing it helped to remind him what he was and what he would always be—a destroyer of worlds. Taking Reece's place just might have changed future history enough to save this world called Earth as well as Reece himself. Tarel certainly hoped that would be the outcome. Maybe then the voices of the dead that echoed in his mind would get even quieter. Tarel had no delusions that they would ever go away.

There had been too many—far too many. Tarel knew he could never completely leave the service of the Klebba until he had silenced all of those voices. With Reece's help, he could maybe silence a few more.

If things went right, Reece would reach his true potential quickly, and return to this place, this time, and this body, so he could return to his the safety of the twisted mass Tarel usually wore. Tarel was afraid if he stayed too long in the handsome, well-constructed flesh he now wore, he would forget the price he owed. It was too late for him to ever be completely forgiven, at least by himself. But Reece—there was still hope for Reece. Tarel just hoped Reece wouldn't do anything stupid. Reece had a lot to learn, and the Klebba were just the creatures to teach him as they had taught Tarel. He reached for the phone to call Julie and reassure her that everything was all right.

About the Author

Susan Satterfield graduated in 2001 with a Masters Degree in English from Central Missouri State University in Warrensburg, Missouri.   Currently, Susan teaches at Longview Community College. She lives in Lee's Summit, Missouri with her extended family including two dogs, five cats, and assorted fish. A long time member of the Kansas City Science Fiction and Fantasy Society, Susan has been an active fan since 1977.

She is the author of three published stories, "Mirror of His Soul" and "The Changing," both appearing in *Eldritch Tales*. Her third published story, A Perfect World," appeared in the Yard Dog Press anthology *Stories That Won't Make Your Parents Hurl* in November of 2000. Currently, Susan is working on other stories set in the *Mirror Images* universe.

About the Artist
Rick Tinney

Art comes easy to children, as we can all witness. It is the natural and logical extension of imaginative play. Somewhere along the way I am sure I was given some simple praise for a crayon scribble and "nature" reared its head and took its course. Now many years later the creation of art is critical maintenance for my self worth, and an indispensable tool for interpreting chaotic thought. Fortunately both are excellent motivators for a prolific work ethic, which I believe is essential for self-evolution as an artist.

I received a Bachelors of Fine Arts degree from Central Missouri State University in 2000. Since graduating I have been working as a graphic artist in order to make a living while promoting my fine arts, and taking on some commissioned paintings. I am also involved in a Kansas City based non-profit studio called, Foresight Fine Arts Studio, Inc.

"Mirror Images: Adventures in Time and Space" is my first book cover, and it has been very exciting and interesting working on the project. Prior to being asked to do the cover it had never actually occurred to me how daunting the task of representing an entire book with one small piece of art could be. However with such a wonderful subject inspiration was easy to find.

Yard Dog Press Titles As Of This Print Date

The Green Women, Laura J. Underwood

The Guardians, Lynn Abbey

Hammer Town, Selina Rosen

The Happiness Box, Beverly A. Hale

The Host Series: The Host, Fright Eater, Gang Approval, Selina Rosen

Houston, We've Got Bubbas!, Edited by Selina Rosen

How I Spent the Apocolypse, Selina Rosen

I Didn't Quite Make It To Oz, Edited by Selina Rosen

I Should Have Stayed In Oz, Edited by Selina Rosen

In the Shadows, Bradley H. Sinor

International House of Bubbas, Edited by Selina Rosen

It's the Great Bumpkin, Cletus Brown!, Katherine A. Turski

The Killswitch Review, Steven-Elliot Altman & Diane DeKelb-
    Rittenhouse

The Leopard's Daughter, Lee Killough

The Lightning Horse, John Moore

The Logic of Departure, Mark W. Tiedemann

The Long, Cold Walk To Mars, Jeffrey Turner

Marking the Signs and Other Tales Of Mischief, Laura J. Underwood

Material Things, Selina Rosen

Medieval Misfits: Renaissance Rejects, Tracy S. Morris

Mirror Images, Susan Satterfield

Mirror, Mirror and Other Reflections, James K. Burk

More Stories That Won't Make Your Parents Hurl, Edited by Selina
    Rosen

Music for Four Hands, Louis Antonelli & Edward Morris

My Life with Geeks and Freaks, Claudia Christian

The Necronomicrap: A Guide To Your Horoooscope, Tim Frayser

Playing With Secrets, Bradley H & Sue P. Sinor

Redheads In Love, Linda L. Donahue, Rhonda Eudaly, Julia S.
    Mandala, & Dusty Rainbolt

Reruns, Selina Rosen

Rock 'n' Roll Universe, Ken Rand

Shadows In Green, Richard Dansky

Stories That Won't Make Your Parents Hurl, Edited by Selina Rosen

Tales from Keltora, Laura J. Underwood

*Tales Of the Lucky Nickel Saloon, Second Ave., Laramie, Wyoming, U
    S of A,* Ken Rand

Tarbox Station, Rhonda Eudaly

Texistani: Indo-Pak Food From A Texas Kitchen, Beverly A. Hale

That's All Folks, J. F. Gonzalez

Through Wyoming Eyes, Ken Rand

Turn Left to Tomorrow, Robin Wayne Bailey

The Twins, Selina Rosen

Wandering Lark, Laura J. Underwood

Wings of Morning, Katharine Eliska Kimbriel

Double Dog (A YDP Imprint):

#1:
Of Stars & Shadows, Mark W. Tiedemann
This Instance Of Me, Jeffrey Turner

#2:
Gods and Other Children, Bill D. Allen
Tranquility, Tracy Morris

#3:
Home Is the Hunter, James K. Burk
Farstep Station, Lazette Gifford

#4:
Sabre Dance, Melanie Fletcher
The Lunari Mask, Laura J. Underwood

#5:
House of Doors, Julia Mandala
Jaguar Moon, Linda A. Donahue

Just Cause (A YDP Imprint):

The Bitter End
Selina Rosen

Death Under the Crescent Moon
Dusty Rainbolt

The Ghost Writer
Selina Rosen

It's Not Rocket Science: Spirituality for the Working-Class Soul
Selina Rosen

Meditations of a Hoarder
Melinda LaFevers

Not My Life
Selina Rosen

The Pit
Selina Rosen

Plots and Protagonists: A Reference Guide for Writers
Mel. White

Vanishing Fame
Selina Rosen

Non-YDP titles we distribute:

Chains of Freedom
Chains of Destruction
Jabone's Sword
Queen of Denial
Recycled
Strange Robby
Sword Masters
Selina Rosen

Three Ways to Order:

1. Write us a letter telling us what you want, then send it along with your check or money order (made payable to Yard Dog Press) to: Yard Dog Press, 710 W. Redbud Lane, Alma, AR 72921-7247

2. Use selinarosen@cox.net or lynnstran@cox.net to contact us and place your order. Then send your check or money order to the address above. *This has the advantage of allowing you to check on the availability of short-stock items such as T-shirts and back-issues of Yard Dog Comics.*

3. Contact us as in #1 or #2 above and pay with a credit card or by debit from your checking account. Either give us the credit card information in your letter/ Email/phone call, or go to our website and use our shopping carts. If you send us your information, please include your name as it appears on the card, your credit card number, the expiration date, and the 3 or 4-digit security code after your signature on the back (CVV). Please remember that we will include media rate (minimum $3.00) S/H for mailing in the lower 48 states.

Watch our website at
www.yarddogpress.com
for news of upcoming projects
and new titles!!

A Note to Our Readers

We at Yard Dog Press understand that many people buy used books because they simply can't afford new ones. That said, and understanding that not everyone is made of money, we'd like you to know something that you may not have realized. Writers only make money on new books that sell. At the big houses a writer's entire future can hinge on the number of books they sell. While this isn't the case at Yard Dog Press, the honest truth is that when you sell or trade your book or let many people read it, the writer and the publishing house aren't making any money.

As much as we'd all like to believe that we can exist on love and sweet potato pie, the truth is we all need money to buy the things essential to our daily lives. Writers and publishers are no different.

We realize that these "freebies" and cheap books often turn people on to new writers and books that they wouldn't otherwise read. However we hope that you will reconsider selling your copy, and that if you trade it or let your friends borrow it, you also pass on the information that if they really like the author's work they should consider buying one of their books at full price sometime so that the writer can afford to continue to write work that entertains you.

We appreciate all our readers and *depend* upon their support.

Thanks,
The Editorial Staff
Yard Dog Press

PS – Please note that "used" books without covers have, in most cases, been stolen. Neither the author nor the publisher has made any money on these books because they were supposed to be pulped for lack of sales.

Please do not purchase books without covers.

www.ingramcontent.com/pod-product-compliance
Lightning Source LLC
Chambersburg PA
CBHW030523130626
46549CB00007B/3077